Dear Parents:

Congratulations! Your child is taking the first steps on an exciting journey. The destination? Independent reading!

STEP INTO READING® will help your child get there. The program offers five steps to reading success. Each step includes fun stories and colorful art or photographs. In addition to original fiction and books with favorite characters, there are Step into Reading Non-Fiction Readers, Phonics Readers and Boxed Sets, Sticker Readers, and Comic Readers—a complete literacy program with something to interest every child.

Learning to Read, Step by Step!

Ready to Read Preschool–Kindergarten
• big type and easy words • rhyme and rhythm • picture clues
For children who know the alphabet and are eager to begin reading.

Reading with Help Preschool–Grade 1
• basic vocabulary • short sentences • simple stories
For children who recognize familiar words and sound out new words with help.

Reading on Your Own Grades 1–3
• engaging characters • easy-to-follow plots • popular topics
For children who are ready to read on their own.

Reading Paragraphs Grades 2–3
• challenging vocabulary • short paragraphs • exciting stories
For newly independent readers who read simple sentences with confidence.

Ready for Chapters Grades 2–4
• chapters • longer paragraphs • full-color art
For children who want to take the plunge into chapter books but still like colorful pictures.

STEP INTO READING® is designed to give every child a successful reading experience. The grade levels are only guides; children will progress through the steps at their own speed, developing confidence in their reading

Remember, a lifetime love of reading starts with a single step!

BARBIE and associated trademarks and trade dress are owned by, and used under license from, Mattel.
©2020 Mattel.
www.barbie.com
Published in the United States by Random House Children's Books, a division of Penguin Random House LLC, 1745 Broadway, New York, NY 10019, and in Canada by Penguin Random House Canada Limited, Toronto.

Step into Reading, Random House, and the Random House colophon are registered trademarks of Penguin Random House LLC.

Visit us on the Web!
StepIntoReading.com
rhcbooks.com

Educators and librarians, for a variety of teaching tools, visit us at RHTeachersLibrarians.com

ISBN 978-0-593-17861-4 (trade) — ISBN 978-0-593-17862-1 (lib. bdg.)

Printed in the United States of America
10 9 8 7 6 5 4 3 2 1

by Elle Stephens

based on a story by Ann Austen

illustrated by Fernando Güell,
Ferran Rodriguez, and David Güell

Random House 🏠 New York

Meet Princess Amelia!
She lives in Floravia.
She has a horse
named Morning Star.

Soon Amelia will be queen.
She has many royal duties.
Sometimes she wants
to be alone.

This is Barbie.

She makes a new video

for her vlog.

Daisy and Chelsea help.

Princess Amelia watches Barbie's vlog. She wants to be like Barbie.

At school,
Barbie and her friends
win a trip to Floravia.
They are so excited!

Barbie hugs her family
at the airport.
Her puppy, Taffy,
sneaks into her bag!

Barbie and her friends
arrive in Floravia.
They will stay
at the royal palace.

Barbie and Taffy
meet Princess Amelia
and her bunny, Snowy.
The girls look alike!

They switch places.
Amelia dresses like
Barbie.
She sneaks out
of the palace.

Barbie dresses like Amelia.

She goes to a royal party.

She meets Prince Johan.

Alonso, the
royal advisor, sees
Barbie's necklace.
He knows she is not
Princess Amelia.

Barbie calls Amelia
to tell her.
Amelia does not want to
go back to the palace yet.

Amelia likes being Barbie.
She goes to the park.
She talks to people
about Floravia.

Barbie agrees to keep
being the princess.
She rides Morning Star
at a royal horse show.

On a walk,
Snowy hops away
from Princess Amelia.
Two footmen see them!

That night,
Snowy finds Barbie
at the palace.
The princess is missing!

Snowy leads Barbie and her friends down a secret passage.

The royal footmen
are inside.
They have
Princess Amelia!
She is in trouble.

Barbie will help.
She finds out
that the footmen work
for Prince Johan.

He wants to be king.

He is hiding Amelia

on his boat to stop her

from being queen.

Barbie rides
Morning Star out
of the palace.
They go to the boat.

Barbie and her friends
find Princess Amelia.
They help her escape
from the boat.

They get to the palace
just in time.
Johan is about
to be crowned king!

Taffy knocks him down.

Barbie catches the crown.

Amelia tells everyone

the truth.

Later that day,
the real Princess Amelia
is crowned queen.

Barbie and her friends
watch.

Everyone claps and cheers.

30

That night, there is a party.

Queen Amelia thanks Barbie.

The new friends hug.

Barbie shares the
party on her vlog
for the world to see!